Victoria's Baby Girl

An MDLG and ABDL lesbian tale of a MTF transgender Police Officer who saves her baby girl in more ways than one

By Tina Moore

Table of Content

Chapter 1

I come from the side of town that good parents warn their kids about, and the stories are all true. We fight for fun and money; your Mum could also be your sister because you're Dad's a fucking rapist, and we drop out of school before we have learned anything that's going to help us go out of this shit hole. But the one thing they don't tell you is just how important loyalty is to us. Maybe it's because it's all we've got and when that's given, and blood is shed to prove it, it's the strongest bond you could imagine. So there we were a bunch of street kids who joined together for one reason or another. I intended to escape the violent outbursts of my Uncle, who had taken to using me as a punching bag for boxing practice. He'd come home drunk and throw some fists, usually passing out before any real damage could be done. I considered myself pretty lucky. Another girl called Hope hung around with us for a while so she wouldn't be fucked by her sister's boyfriend, but he had already forced himself on her a couple of times.

We spent our time throwing stones at each other, standing around on corners glaring at the people who walked by, drinking in parks, and running from cops. We'd break into stores and steal candy and condoms, and knew all the best hideouts where we'd wait while the cops ran around looking for us. I couldn't even count the times Victoria caught me. We all just called her Vicki for short, she was our favorite cop, and I'd grown up running from her. She would chase the gang and me over fences and under bridges. She'd always catch one of us, throw us into the backseat of the car, hands cuffed behind our backs. She'd try all the tricks to get us to rat out the other people involved. Saying things like, "We already have it all on CCTV so you might as well do yourself a favor and try for a lesser sentence," or "I won't be able to help you if this gets pushed further up the chain, you know what happens next." But I would always laugh or respond with, "No comment," and she would have no choice but to let me go after 24 hours. She was the only cop who had ever caught any of us, and sometimes, we'd even wait for her to be on duty before we robbed a store so that she'd chase us. She wasn't like the other cops. They were pretty dumb, and we could easily give them the slip. But not Vicki. She would hunt us down for hours, making us run until we thought our lungs would give out. But when she caught one of us, which she always did, she was nice and kind and made us feel kinda like shit for ripping off the store manager. She'd make us go around there and apologize, hitting us over the head if she didn't think we were sincere enough. She knew we'd never call her out on 'Police Brutality,' despite her strength and size, she wasn't brutal at all. Her arms were full sleeves of ink, and her shoulders were broader than any woman's I had ever seen. She stood tall, taller than most of the men in town, and when she walked down the sidewalk, people had to move out of her way, or they'd be knocked to the ground by accident. I thought she was gorgeous, but I never admitted that to the guys. I just found myself letting her catch me as I got older, just excited to be near her.

But I had stepped away from the gang a little bit now that I wasn't a minor anymore. Now, if I got caught doing the shit we use to do, I'd be given a much bigger sentence maybe even jail time, and the thought of that didn't thrill me. I did miss those days, though. Now I work at a local store in town selling furniture during the week and getting drunk on the weekends. It a pretty basic and boring life, but at least I wasn't a Mum or in jail. My 21st was fast approaching, and I had invited a couple of the old gang over for some drinks on the weekend. I'd gone to buy some party supplies and was on my way out of the store, looking into the bag of candy and glitter I had just bought when I felt a familiar arm almost knock me over.

"Oi Vicki," I said, looking up at the muscled arms she used to use to pin me to the ground. She had done that so many times I had a scar under my chin from the repeated gravel rash I sported during my late teens.

"Where's your mates. I haven't seen you around them in a while," Vicki said, looking over my head and into the store.

"Show me the receipt," she added, grabbing the bag.

"Hey," I said, trying to pull away from her. Vicki just raised an eyebrow, but I hardly saw it because I didn't want to meet her eyes. I was embarrassed about what I had just bought. I reached into the bag and took out the receipt before passing it to her and looking down at the ground.

"Are you having a party?" Vicki asked, suddenly sounding kinder. I nodded and reached for the receipt.

"I'm turning 21 tomorrow," I whispered and tried to sidestep Vicki, but she moved before I could and blocked my way.

"Hey, happy birthday for tomorrow Ava, it'll be nice not to have to kick you out of bars anymore," Vicki said kindly. I looked up at her and gave her a sideward smile and walked out of the store. *Damn, why does she have to smell so good,* I thought to myself stepping past her quickly as I felt my face begin to turn red. That was the last thing I needed, her seeing what she could do to me.

Chapter 2

"Happy birthday, bitch," Hope said, handing me a drink and a slice of pizza. I laughed, and we danced around my kitchen while the guys played beer pong in the living room. It was almost midnight when we heard a knock at the front door, and we all looked at each other. Everyone that was supposed to be here was. It wasn't uncommon for people to crash parties and steal a whole lot of stuff, so I grabbed a kitchen knife, and the others followed suit. I approached the door and felt myself square up, ready to attack any intruder. Opening the door aggressively, I held the knife up in front of my face.

"What!" I yelled angrily but bringing the knife down when I saw her standing in front of me. She had some dude standing behind her, and I liked that she silenced him when he started to have a go at me for threatening Police.

"How could I be threatening you when I didn't even know you where there fuckwit," I said back as Vicki pushed her way in and rolled her eyes. She looked around the room before she turned back to me.

"Any minors?" She asked as the other cop circled behind me, making me feel uncomfortable.

"No, do you think I'm stupid?" I replied, taking a step

forward to get away from the cop at my back.

"We've had noise complaints, Ava, I need you to turn the music down," Vicki said sitting on the couch.

"Comfy," she said, bouncing slightly. One of my mates, Connor, laughed.

"Ava? Vicki, I didn't know we are all on a first-name basis," he said making the other cop angry.

"We're not. It'll be Constable to you," he said, shoving his baton in Connor's chest. Connor scoffed, pushing it away and took a step back.

"Just keep it down, yeah?" Vicki said, standing up and coming over to me. I could feel everyone's eyes on me as she paused in front of me and put her hand on the small of my back. She eyed me up and down, taking in my short dress and heels. Her eyes twinkled, and I had to catch my breath as she smiled at me in a way that no one ever had before. She winked at me before walking out, closing the door behind her.

"What in all of hell was that about?" Hope squealed.

"Are you fucking her?" Connor said, and I shook my head and went back to the kitchen, grabbed a bottle of whiskey, and jumped out the kitchen window. I made my way down the fire escape and onto the street, but my legs took over, and I was running before I knew it. I didn't know where I was running, too, but I just had to get out of there. *Fuck, fuck, fuck,* was all I could think as I made my way to the park and found a spot under the bridge. I opened the bottle and drank as much as my body could hold in one go before swallowing and almost throwing it all back up.

"What's a pretty girl like you doing here all alone?" A man's voice said, waking me up. It was early dawn, and the water by the river was beginning to glisten. I got up wanting to leave, but he pulled me back down and onto his lap. I could feel him easily under my short dress, and he reached around to try and rub me through my panties. I elbowed him in the face and scrambled up the river bank back to where the morning runners were doing their routine exercises. I knew he wouldn't chase me up here, which meant I was safe, so I walked along the path, realizing that I had left my shoes down by the river. *Great, now I look like I'm coming home from a wild night, and all I did was pass out under a bridge,* I thought to myself, pulling a face when I saw Vicki walking towards me.

"Good morning," Vicki said, clearly amused.

"Did you have fun last night?" She added.

"I was having a great time until you showed up," I spat back at her making her stop walking. I wish I hadn't, but I turned around to look at her.

"Look, I'm sorry, just stop being so bloody nice to me, alright, it's got people talking," I tried to explain. Vicki wasn't wearing her uniform, and I hated myself for thinking that her running shorts and singlet looked hot on her. Her shiny black hair was in a loose ponytail, and her short shorts showed off thigh tats I hadn't realized she had. Catching me staring, Vicki crossed her arms, which just made her forearm muscles bulge and made me blush.

"This isn't me being nice, your friends would have something to talk about if I was nice," Vicki said as she placed her hands on her hips. I don't know what came over me, but seeing her like this, hearing her non-Police voice made my head spin. I ran forward, kissed her quickly on the mouth, and turned before I could see her reaction and sprinted towards home. I knew she could catch me if she wanted to, she had always managed to catch me before, but when I didn't hear footsteps coming behind me, I turned to see her standing where I had left her. She extended a finger and motioned for me to come back to her. I stayed looking at her for the longest time, and seeing her reassuring smile, I slowly made my way back to her.

"You want to explain that to me?" Vicki said, sitting down on a park bench. I shook my head and looked at her.

"Well, let me explain it to you. When you kiss someone do it like this," Vicki said, wrapping her arms around my body and pressing the back of my head into her mouth. She ran her fingers through my hair and pressed my mouth harder on her as her tongue parted my lips and explored my mouth. I could hardly breathe, my heart was beating hard against my chest, and I gingerly placed my hands on her thighs as I melted into her. Breaking the kiss, Vicki looked down into my eyes and held my head in both her hands, stroking my cheeks with her thumbs.

"That's how you kiss someone, Ava," Vicki said, kissing the tip of my nose before getting up and walking away.

Chapter 3

My mind had been racing since that kiss. I had gone back to my apartment in a daze, unable to explain what had happened or where I had been. Hope and I had cleaned up after the party, and I had told her I had a headache and needed a nap. In truth, I just wanted some time alone. I had not only kissed Vicki, but she had kissed me. Her touch had been soft but firm, almost protective, and I still had her perfume on my dress. She had whispered in my ear that she'd see me around and I couldn't wait until the next time she saw me. Things would be different; I would be different. I had to become the sort of person she wouldn't be embarrassed to be with. I went to my cupboard and started going through my clothes, throwing out things that looked trashy or cheap. I booked an appointment at the hairdressers to get a fresh color and cut, and I pulled on some activewear and went for a jog around the block.

It had been three months since that first kiss with Vicki when I saw her again, and at first, she didn't recognize me. I had swapped my usual grunge look for something more clean-cut. A pair of dark denim high waist jeans and a white fitted t-shirt tucked in, some tan heeled sandals, and my hair was a Scandi white blonde. I had learned how to apply makeup that wasn't solely black eyeliner, and I had taken to getting a shade of baby pink on my nails at the nail salon. Tonight I had decided to try a new bar that had just opened up on the other side of town but hadn't invited any of my old gang. It wasn't my choice to go alone, but ever since that first kiss, I had lost one friend after another. They didn't like the new me, though that I thought I was better than them or something stupid like that. It hurt me at first, but I had been used to being alone, so I just adapted and had even put in for a promotion at work.

"Mind if I sit?" A voice smoothly said as I sipped my cocktail. I turned my head and saw Vicki standing in front of me. Her eyes grew wide when she realized it was me sitting there.

"Oh my god, Ava?" Vicki asked, still not believing it was me. I giggled and nodded, and Vicki pulled a face I knew meant she was impressed.

"Wow, look at you all grown up," Vicki said, sitting down next to me. I looked around her and saw that some of the other cops were here tonight, probably with her.

"Don't worry, as long as you don't get up to any mischief they'll stay away, I always told you that, but you never listened, did you?" Vicki teased. She got the bar tender's attention and ordered a beer and another cocktail for me making me blush.

"I had no idea you could be so adorable, Ava," Vicki said as she began drinking with me.

"What else has changed?" She added, placing her hand on my thigh and squeezing it sensually. I liked knowing that she wanted me, but I took her hand off my thigh, making her face look confused.

"For one thing, now I make people ask permission before they just take what they want," I said, hoping that Vicki wouldn't be annoyed. She just laughed and nodded in agreement.

"Well, may I?" She asked, holding out her hand as the music in the bar changed to a slow song. I kept her waiting as I finished my drink before accepting her hand, and she led me to the dance floor, twirling me before bring me in and slow dancing with me. Even with my heels on, I was still a head and shoulders shorted than Vicki, which meant my eyes were in line with her breasts, and I held my breath as a fire began to grow inside of me. Wanting to distract myself from my thoughts, I looked up at her to find that she was already looking down at me.

"You're lovely, Ava," Vicki said lovingly, making me wet as she pulled me in closer.

"You've always been lovely," I quietly said, making her smile.

"I knew you thought so, you went from being the hardest to catch to being the easiest overnight, I knew something had to give," Vicki teased twirling me around again, but I let her hand go and walked back over to the safety of the bar.

"Are you alright?" Vicki asked, coming over to join me,

sounding concerned. I shook my head.

"We are from two completely different worlds, don't you understand everyone will think I'm fucking the enemy Vicki," I said. I felt more emotional than I wish I had as a tear escaped my eye. Vicki took my hand in hers and held it softly before speaking.

"Are you worried about what people will think, baby?" Vicki said. I looked up at her, shocked. No one had ever called me baby before; I had always just been a tease, something to fuck. I was about to speak when that cop that Vicki had brought to mine came over.

"Causing any trouble over here," he said, making me roll my eyes.

"Oh please fuck off," I replied, making Vicki laugh, and she placed her hand on his chest, making him stop talking and go back to the group of cops sitting in the back.

"Come on, let's get out of here, baby," Vicki said, taking my hand. I felt my arms tingle as I took her hand and followed her out of the bar, shivering in the cold night air.

"Here," Vicki said, taking off her tan leather jacket and draping it over my shoulders.

"You've done that before," I said, enjoying the weight of her jacket on my shoulders, the arms coming down to my mid-thigh.

"Maybe just once or twice," Vicki said, laughing. We

walked until we found a café that was still opened and she held the door as I walked inside. It was fun being here. These were the types of places I use to rob. Now I was here with the one cop who would have been able to catch me.

"What would like, darling?" Vicki said, running her fingers through my hair. I forced myself to read the menu.

"Just a caramel latte please," I replied, being surprised when Vicki paid, following her as she found a booth away from the other people who were in the café.

"I'll get the next one," I said, not wanting her to think I couldn't pay my way.

"Alright, are you asking me out on a date then?" Vicki teased. I just nodded, and she happily wrapped her arm around me.

"I think this is the start of something very exciting, baby," Vicki said, and we drank our coffees in silence as we watched the world go by outside.

"I've had a wonderful night," I said as Vicki walked me back home. I liked having her by my side. She had held my hand the whole way, and I was seriously considering fucking her tonight. It would have been too easy to let her come up to my apartment and let her have her way with me. But I wanted her to think I was special and not just another slut she could easily have, so I kissed her again at my front door and handed her back her jacket.

"You're going to make me wait?" Vicki said, placing her hand on the front door and pushing her body against mine, making me stumble back, and I had to suppress a moan as she ground into me against the door. I just nodded and bit my bottom lip. She brushed my cheek with the back of her hand, and I suddenly was hugging her, feeling her heartbeat against my face.

"I'm going to try," I softly said, resulting in her kissing the top of my head and giggling.

"Well, I have waited this long, I guess I can wait a little longer," Vicki said before she winked at me and began to walk back out onto the street. I put the key in my door and turned the handle, almost falling inside in a haze of happiness and dizzy excitement.

Chapter 4

"Hi Vicki, it's Ava," I said, trying not to sound as desperate as I felt. I had waited until the next morning before ringing Vicki, and I was excited she had picked up almost instantly.

"Hey, sweetie, how are you?" Vicki replied, making me smile immediately.

"Yeah, good, whad bout ya?" I said kind of annoyed my backwater accent came through. Vicki didn't seem to mind as she began to tell me about a drug bust she had just come from.

"Oh, sorry I didn't realize you were working," I said, kicking myself for being so stupid.

"It's not a problem, baby. What's up?" Vicki said. I could tell she had moved out of the noisy room she had previously been in and wondered what room of the station she was in; I knew almost all of them.

"I was just wondering if you'd want to meet up again?" I said, holding my breath and only exhaling when Vicki replied.

"Yes. When are you free?" Vicki said. We arranged a time to meet, in three days at the museum in town and I hung up the phone, practically dancing on air.

"Hello, sweetness," I heard Vicki say before she came up

behind me and hugged my waist. I loved how small she made me feel. It wasn't just her size; she made me feel so protected and safe when she was around like I could cuddle into her whenever I felt scared or nervous.

"Hi," I said, taken by surprise, and I turned in her arms to feel her mouth on mine before I could say another word. Breaking the kiss, I giggled and held out my hand, which she took in hers as we walked inside.

"I can't believe you've never been to a museum before," Vicki said as we passed a bunch of old-looking stuff. I looked to surprise, making her laugh her deep raspy laugh.

"Shall I explain all these things you've missed?" I said to her stopping to look at something to prove I was into looking at old things, which I most certainly was not. But I liked listening to how educated Vicki was about the things we were looking at. She told me stories about how she had gone to Rome and saw the ruins and to Egypt to see the Pyramids. It made me smile in wonder.

"Where to now?" Vicki asked as we exited the Museum. I looked around the green space that rolled down the hill to the river that wound through the city. I turned to look at Vicki with nothing but pure mischief in my eyes.

"Race ya," I said, tearing off down the hill followed by Vicki, who overtook me, grabbing me and picking me up. She whirled me around in her arms and slowly put me back down, and the whole world faded. All I saw was her as her long black hair was blown by the wind in the late summer afternoon breeze.

"I want you," I said before I kissed her and grazed my fingertips over her breasts. I was surprised, it was the first time she had seemed unsure of herself, and it made me feel nervous.

"Or not, like if you're not into it, that's cool," I said, trying to backpedal, so she didn't have to turn me down. Vicki sat down and looked up at the white clouds that floated by.

"It's not that I don't want to, it's that I am not sure you'll want to," Vicki said softly. I looked at her with a confused expression.

"Um, wasn't I the one who just tried to instigate it?" I said, using a word I had learned only last week, I was quite impressed with myself. Vicki took my hand and pulled me close to her. She put it on her thigh and watched my face as she moved my hand up her thigh and pushed it down onto her crotch. I gasped and pulled away involuntarily and looked up at her in confusion. She just looked plain-faced at me as I put my hand back down on her and felt her over her trousers.

"But," I said before stopping. Vicki cleared her throat before she spoke.

"I'm trans sweetie, I just never had the surgery. I kinda like my dick, so I kept it, having it doesn't make me feel any less female. Everyone is different; this is how I feel," Vicki said. I took my hand away and looked at her.

"Is this a bad time to tell you that I've never," I said.

"Never had sex with a trans woman? That's a pretty common thing never to have done, baby," Vicki said, but I shook my head.

"No, I've never had um, I don't know how to say this without sounding offensive. But I've never fucked a dick before," I said, trying not to hurt Vicki's feelings. I was glad when she smiled.

"Little gold star, hey?" Vicki said.

"I want to, though. With you," I replied, not wanting her to think it was off the table and over between us. Vicki raised an eyebrow.

"Really?" She said, kissing me deeply when I nodded my head.

"Come on, baby girl, let me get you home then," Vicki said, standing to hail a taxi.

"Lay down," Vicki said when we were back in my apartment. It was close, so I had suggested we go there. I lay down on my bed and watched as Vicki slowly took off her clothes. Her pink button-down falling to the floor made my mouth gaped open as she began rubbing her large breasts over her pink bra.

"Do you like what you see?" Vicki said, smirking at my

lustful stare. I swallowed hard and nodded.

"Use your words, baby," Vicki said, making me blush.

"Yes, Vicki," I replied softly, watching as she unzipped her pants. She let them drop to the floor as well and took off her bra before climbing onto the bed with me.

"Come here," Vicki said in a commanding voice. I moved to her, and she picked me up and placed me on her lap facing her. She held me tight as she lifted my t-shirt over my head and groped my smaller tits excitedly. I closed my eyes and melted into her embrace as she pulled off my shorts and panties in one go. Feeling slightly exposed, Vicki noticed and pulled the bed sheets back down, and I climbed into bed followed by Vicki.

"If you want to stop, baby girl, you must tell me, alright?" Vicki said lovingly as I began to feel more confident.

"Yes, Vicki," I said as I began to kiss her and climbed on top of her. She let me place my hands around her neck as my body dropped between her thighs and began to grind on her making her pant in my ear. I could feel she was getting hard, and I liked that I had this power over her.

"Do you like that, Vicki?" I said sweetly, knowing that she was letting me be in control.

"Yes, baby," Vicki moaned before grabbing my body and rolling on top of me.

"Come to Mommy," Vicki moaned, making me freeze.

"Mommy?" I questioned, making Vicki open her eyes

widely, realizing what she had just moaned.

"Um, I," Vicki stammered before I reached down and placed my hand firmly on her dick.

"Mommy, teach me," I said, enjoying the new dynamic she had just slipped us into. Relaxing, Vicki went back to feeling my body and sucked on my nipples, making me giggle.

"God, you're a cute baby girl. You've always been such a cute girl," Vicki said, reaching down and feeling between my thighs.

"Do you like it when Mommy talks to you, baby girl?" Vicki moaned in my ear as I grabbed her firmly and began to push her panties down.

"Oh baby girl, rub it for Mommy," Vicki said as I began to jerk her off.

"Just like that, good girl, tell Mommy you want it," Vicki said, making me moan as she flicked my clit over and over.

"Mommy, I want it," I moaned, feeling Vicki fill my tight pussy with her finger.

"Louder," Vicki commanded, forcing my pussy open with another finger.

"Mommy, please fuck me, I want it," I squealed as Vicki pumped my pussy making me cum. She suddenly jumped up and pinned my two wrists above my head with one hand as she guided her dick into my virgin pussy.

"Mommy," I breathed, feeling her fill me. She stayed

inside of me until my muscles relaxed around her before she slowly pulled out of me to push back in with a little more force.

"There you go, baby girl; you're going to get fucked by Mommy sweetheart. Hold onto Mommy baby," Vicki said, lowering herself on me and letting my wrists go. I wrapped my arms around her as she gently fucked me. I loved having such a powerful woman be so gentle with me, and I began to suck my thumb, which delighted Vicki.

"Such a cute little girl getting taken by Mommy, you're going to cum for Mommy baby," Vicki said, beginning to fuck me harder. She reached down and cupped herself as she pushed her dick hard against my hilt taking her other hand and pressing down on my pelvis, making me feel her deeper inside of me.

"Mommy, please," I moaned, feeling my cum around her dick, getting long strokes from her as she edged herself.

"Oh good girl," Vicki said, pulling out of me and cumming on my tummy. She surged through her hand and covered me until she was finished, stroking my hair with her other hand, her strong thighs keeping her over me.

"Baby girl, oh that was the best Mommy has had in a long time, thank you," Vicki said as I began to tear up.

"Oh, sweetie, did I hurt you?" Vicki said, suddenly worried. I just shook my head no, and she held me as I hyperventilated, and tears rolled down my cheeks.

"Talk to me, baby girl," Vicki said lovingly when I began to calm down.

"It was just a lot, Mommy," I replied, hoping Vicki was happy to be called Mommy even after sex. She smiled down at me and patted my bottom gently.

"Sorry, I should have told you I cum hard," Vicki said, missing my meaning.

"No, Mommy, it was like, better than I have ever had. You've blown my mind," I replied, kissing her arm softly. Vicki took me to the bathroom and washed me clean before she carried me back out into the living room and sat me down on the couch with her. It was the first time that I had seen her dick, and I was surprised she had fit it all inside of me, she was big and still hard, which made me surprised.

"I can put my clothes back on if it's a problem," Vicki said, catching me looking intensely at her.

"Oh no, Mommy, I just like, it's all so new and big," I replied, making her laugh and look down.

"Yeah, I suppose it is, but I'm kinda big too, so anything smaller would look weird I guess," Vicki replied, making a tea and bringing it over to me.

"Here, little girl," Vicki said. I sipped the tea and let the stream of thoughts run through my mind as we drank in silence. I imagined her bending me over the kitchen table and ramming into me, pulling my hair back as she came, forcing herself in my ass and filling it with her cum. Breaking my thoughts, I shook my head and looked at Vicki, who had begun flicking through her phone.

"So, does this make me your girlfriend?" I said, grimacing at how stupid I sounded. Vicki just laughed.

"Do you want to be my girlfriend?" Vicki asked, putting her phone down and repositioning herself. I looked at her like she just asked the dumbest thing in the world.

"Yeah, of course, are you lost? I've always wanted to be your girlfriend!" I said, putting my tea down before crawling into Vicki's lap.

"Oh baby careful, now you're asking for it," Vicki said as I felt her hardening against my ass.

Chapter 5

Vicki stayed the night, but we had agreed to meet up in a few days, she was going to cook me dinner. I felt the work week drag on and was happy to be coming home on Friday afternoon. I stopped in on the way home and picked up a bottle of wine to have with dinner and smiled as I saw a group of teens standing outside the bottle shop asking people if they would buy them alcohol. I remembered doing that with my mates just four years ago, but it felt like yesterday. I passed the kids but stopped when they started talking to me.

"Can you buy just anything, Miss?" One of the older looking girls said. I looked at her, and she looked familiar.

"No, sorry, you know I can't. Hey, you're Hope's sister, aren't you?" I asked. Now I knew where I had seen her before. She was about to reply when I saw her friends scurry off behind her, and a shadow fell across her face. Confused, I turned around to see Vicki in full uniform standing behind us.

"Hello there, haven't you got somewhere to be, like somewhere doing homework?" Vicki said to the girl who just scoffed and walked back slowly before turning on her heel and bolting after her friends. I laughed.

"Same old Vicki," I said, reaching up to cuddle her, but she pushed me away, making my heart ache instantly.

"Not now, sweetie," Vicki said. She had started to say something else, but I didn't hear it. I was walking away from her, having her rejection was too painful to stand around and hear her reasons why.

I was almost back at my car when I heard her footsteps coming behind me.

"Hey, come here," Vicki said, opening her arms just for me to push her away.

"No, not now, sweetie," I mocked, trying to hold back my tears.

"Baby, Mommy has to be a certain way when I'm at work. I'm sorry you felt unloved. It's not that at all, baby girl," Vicki said softly so no one but us could hear. She looked around before reaching down and cupping my chin in her hand she forced me to look at her.

"Ava, you know you're my good girl, I should have told you the rules for when Mommy is working baby, I'm sorry," Vicki said making me annoyed I could feel soothed by her so easily. I nodded, and she wiped the last of my tears away before opening my door for me.

"You really should be more careful about locking your car, baby," Vicki said, frowning.

"Who is going to try and rob me? I may not get into any trouble now, but they all know I can beat a bitch down," I replied, making Vicki smirk and grab my upper arm.

"My tough little princess," she teased, making me laugh as I got into my car and before to drive away.

Walking up to my apartment, I knew something was wrong straight away. The opened door was a pretty big give away since I knew I had locked it this morning.

"Hello?" I said, slowly opening the door and peering inside. The house had been ripped apart, looking like the typical robbery scene. Couch cushions were all over the floor, and candles, photo frames, and appliances where all broken and scattering around the living room. One of the walls had a spray-painted 'Cop fucker' written in black paint, and the other wall had 'Five-O Homo' in red and blue. My TV had been stolen, as well as my laptop and camera equipment. I had been relatively calm until I walked into the bedroom and found them. The group of kids that had been outside the bottle shop, but this time they had traded in their bikes for baseball bats. There were four of them; I was happy. Hope's sister wasn't one of them. But there was only one of me, and I knew this was about to get ugly. The thing about growing up here was that this wasn't my first break-in and it certainly wasn't my first fight. The rules of a fight around here are pretty simple. If someone tries to beat you down, make sure you don't lose. These kids were about 18 years old but out here that didn't matter, I wasn't about to go easy on them, and I slowly put my bag down.

"Do you like to fuck cops, hey?" The first person to speak in a gang is always the leader, so now I knew who to hit first. I looked around at them and felt the old me come through my eyes. They use to call me wild cat because of the way furry burned in my eyes when I fought, and I could see by the fear growing in one of the other guys that I hadn't lost my touch.

"Yeah, what of it, cunt?" I replied, spitting at them. The leader laughed and swung the bat, but I blocked him before he could hit me and punched my fist into his mouth, knocking a tooth out and sending him backward. I stopped and looked around to see the other three who had stepped back when I stepped to them.

"I thought you bitches wanted a fight?" I yelled, grabbing a bat off one of them and swinging into another's knee cap. I wasn't about to see if they were going to back up their threats; they should have known not to fuck with me. I heard a baby cry as their leader got up and tried to swing at me again, but this time I used the bat as a ramming stick and made him double over as his dick was hit.

"Get the fuck out," I yelled, making the two uninjured boys bolt for my door. I grabbed the boy I had hit over his knee cap by the ear and enjoyed feeling him wince in pain as I threw him out before going back to get their leader.

"Come around here again, next time I'll be packing so we

can play target practice you useless mother fucker," I viciously whispered in his ear before kicking his ass as I pushed him out the door, slamming it behind him. I fell to the floor and began shaking and crying. I pulled my legs to my chest and muffled my screams as I felt my body shake with fear and sadness. I stayed there, my back to the door until Vicki was calling my phone. I had completely forgotten that I was meant to be having dinner with her tonight.

"Hey baby, just wondering if you are on your way?" Vicki said lovingly. I hadn't stopped crying for hours, and I knew my voice would give me away.

"I'm sorry, I lost track of time, I," I replied before getting cut off.

"What's wrong, baby?" Vicki said. I didn't know how to reply. I looked around my apartment and felt embarrassed. Embarrassed that I thought I could have a life with her, embarrassed that I had to go back to old ways to stay safe, but mostly I was embarrassed, I was ruining my chances with her.

"Sweetie?" Vicki said, breaking my thoughts.

"I can't do this," I said softly, making her go quiet on the phone.

"Alright," Vicki said, which just made me cry again.

"I'm coming over baby, will you let me come over," Vicki said making me surprised she wasn't giving up on me. I looked around my apartment, and I couldn't care, she would see it if she wanted too.

"Yep, OK," I said before hanging up the phone.

It wasn't more than 20minutes later when a knock came from the door, and I pulled myself up to open the door for Vicki.

"Baby come here," she said as soon as she saw me. She pulled me in tight and held me, making me cry all over again. I was getting sick of all this crying; it had started to give me a headache.

"What the fuck?" Vicki said she had seen the apartment. She looked down at me.

"Are you alright? Did you get hurt?" Vicki said, starting to look me over, making me laugh.

"No, I won, Vicki, you know I always win," I replied. Vicki picked me up, and I wrapped my legs around her waist.

"Mommy," Vicki said correcting me and I snuggled into her before repeating,

"Mommy," into her neck. She smelt like her usual sweet perfume, and I breathed

her in deeply, wanting all of her.

"Tell me what happened, baby girl," Vicki said, clearing a spot on the couch and sitting me on her lap while looking around the room.

"I came home, and the door was open," I said before getting cut off.

"So, you thought you'd go inside and not call Mommy?!"

Vicki said shocked I wouldn't think to call her.

"Well, yeah," I replied honestly.

"Mommy, you know how things like this go," I replied, putting my fingers to her lips playfully before continuing.

"Then I saw all of this, and when I went into my bedroom, four guys were standing there with bats, but I took one of them and kicked them out. Nothing bad happened, but my place is trashed," I said, cuddling into her. She wrapped an arm around me and patted my back as I snuggled.

"Cop fucker, original," Vicki said, but I could tell she was angry, I could feel it in her pulse, her blood was pumping quicker, and her face was stern.

"I understand why you wanted to call it off, baby. But I don't want you too," Vicki said, looking at me with a seriousness I knew all too well.

"I don't want to either, it was just a lot, I went kinda feral on those guys, and I hate to admit it, but I was a little shook," I said putting my hands down into her lap. Vicki raised an eyebrow at me as I began to pat and rub over her jeans.

"Now, you want to play now? After everything that has happened?" Vicki said, repositioning herself and biting her bottom lip.

"Yeah, why not?" I said a little disappointed when Vicki shook her head no.

"You don't owe me, baby," Vicki said, making me annoyed

she could read me so easily.

"But I don't know how else to thank you for being so lovely," I said softly, looking at her getting hard, wondering how she could have so much self-control.

"How about you pack a bag and come and stay at mine over the weekend instead of staying here? We can come back tomorrow and clean it up. I doubt you'll get your gear back, but do you have insurance?" Vicki said. I got up, and Vicki followed me into my bedroom and sat on my bed.

"Yeah, I do. I'll probs get something back from them, right?" I asked. I had never filled out an insurance claim before. I'd only got insurance because the employers at my job made everyone have some. I had thought it was a waste of money until right now.

"I'll help you with it, it can be tricky," Vicki said, helping me pack.

"You won't need these," Vicki said, taking out my panties. I looked at her, confused.

"I don't like wearing no panties, even when I'm at home," I said to a laughing Vicki.

"Oh, you'll be covered don't worry, but it won't be with panties," Vicki said smirking and playfully spanking my ass. I shook it for her, and she grabbed my hips and roughly pulled me down on her making me sit on her lap.

"Don't tease Mommy baby girl, there's only so much

control I have," Vicki whispered in my ear as she flicked my nipples, making me squirm and moan on her lap.

"Yes, shake that little ass for Mommy," Vicki said, slapping my ass firmly, making me jump.

"Oh, Mommy's sensitive little girl," Vicki said slowly as she pushed a finger into my mouth and grabbed the crotch of my shorts, pulling it to the side. I could feel her getting hard under me, and I bounced on her lap, wet with excitement. Vicki took her finger out of me and slide it up and down my wet slit, teasing me and holding me in place with her legs wrapped around mine, forcing them open.

"Do you like it when I hold you like this baby?" Vicki said, grabbing my tit and shaking it in her hand.

"Does Mommy make you feel safe?" She continued, smiling as I moaned in response. She did make me feel safe, she made me feel like nothing could ever hurt me again, and she knew it. I bucked against her hand, she had made me cum more times than I could count, and I needed her to stop.

"You can't get away from Mommy, baby. I'm too strong for you to escape me," Vicki said as she bit down on my neck. I felt her lift me and when she put me back down, she slid me onto her big dick and filled my used pussy, holding me in the air as she fucked me. She pounded into me as I tried to escape her, enjoying how her grip only tightened on my thighs.

"Don't you fucking dare move little girl, you'll take

Mommy as long as I want you too," Vicki growled, as she dropped me on her lap and pushed me forward. She pushed my body down on the bed. She pinned me there, grabbed my shorts by the crotch again, and rammed back into me, slapping my ass when I tried to fight her.

"What did Mommy say about that princess?" Vicki moaned as she pulled out and turned me over before pushing her cumming dick into my mouth.

"Suck it, baby girl, let Mommy use you," Vicki said as I swallowed her, gagging as she poured down my throat. She smiled as she saw her cum spilling from my mouth and pulled out slightly when my eyes started to water and stroked my cheek while pushing her dick along the side of my mouth.

"Cute baby," Vicki said as she took it out of my mouth and pulled me in for a cuddle.

"I love you, Mommy," I said as she held me against her breast and let me fall asleep in her arms.

Chapter 6

When we finally got to hers, it was late, and I was tired. We had fucked for hours at mine, and I had happily let Vicki use me as I lay exhausted and limp on my bed. Her stamina was incredible. She had practically carried me to her car and buckled me in, putting a blankie over the top of me and let me drift in and out of sleep as she drove us to her home.

"We're here, darling," Vicki said, gently shaking me awake. I opened my eyes and looked around. We lived in different suburbs. The streets here were like something from a movie. The street was lined with tall leafy trees and the houses where big colonial-style homes with perfect gardens and sidewalks. Vicki came around to the passenger side and opened the door for me and helped me down from her big SUV. I liked her car, it had cream leather and wood trim, and the navy blue paint was always clean. She grabbed my backpack and took me inside. Her home was modern, and I was surprised that a cop could afford something like this. She must have seen my face because she laughed as she shut the door behind me.

"I wasn't always a cop baby," Vicki said, leading me through the house. Her bedroom was as big as my entire apartment and looked out over the manicured back yard.

"Why are you even messing with me?" I said to her, feeling stupid and out of place her in her luxury home. Vicki frowned and came over to me, making me feel even smaller.

"Baby, I'm not *messing* with you. I loving on you," Vicki said, grabbing me and holding me tight.

"But like, what can I even offer you, like, I can't match this!" I said, pulling away from her and letting the house overwhelm me. Vicki laughed and walked into the kitchen. Worried that I would get lost, I quickly followed her.

"Let me explain something to you, baby girl because you have a few things mixed up. I don't need you to match this, I need you to be your cute, baby self and let Mommy take care of you," Vicki said, passing me a drink in a sippy cup. I looked at it and looked at her, rolling my eyes.

"If you're going to be a brat, Mommy can spank you if you'd like?" Vicki said, making me giggle as she pushed the drink into my hands.

"No, Mommy," I said, drinking obediently. Vicki got herself a wine and went into the bathroom.

"Bathies baby girl," she said, reaching down to pick me up.

"Hey, I can walk," I said, wriggling out of her grasp.

"You'll let Mommy carry you, or you'll crawl my darling," Vicki said, smiling victoriously when I reluctantly lifted my arms, accepting her embrace.

"Good girl," Vicki said, taking me into the bathroom. She ran a bath and undressed me before helping me into the bath.

"Mommy, are you coming?" I asked, making Vicki smile.

"Would you like me to, baby?" She asked, taking off her shoes. I nodded and watched as she undressed and sat down on the opposite end of the bath.

"So, Mommy, is that for me?" I asked, pointing to the diaper and clothes Vicki had placed on the counter. She turned to see what I was pointing at, turning back and moved over to where I was sitting. I moved into her arms and loved how she kissed me softly, smiling when I moaned between kisses.

"Yes, baby," Vicki said before washing me clean. I enjoyed that she was so gentle on my cunt, I could still feel her in me and flinched, thinking she would be rough.

"You don't need to be scared of me sweetie, Mommy isn't going to hurt you," she said before getting out and drying herself.

"You are going to look so cute in these baby," Vicki said, taking my hand and pulling me out of the bath. She put a duck hooded towel over my head before she playfully dried me off, making she giggle and squirm under her touch.

"Stay still for me, little one," Vicki said, putting a pacifier in my mouth. I froze, I don't think anyone had ever given me one before. Vicki must have sensed my shock and pulled me to the floor, she had placed a clean, dry towel down, and I followed her instruction and spread my legs and lifted my bottom.

"It's OK baby, Mommy is here now, and I'm going to give you all the loving you could ever need," Vicki said placing a hand on my tummy and gently pressing down.

"Come on, let's fill this little tummy of yours," she said, picking me up and carrying me back to the kitchen.

"Mommy," I whispered in her ear from behind my new pink paci. Vicki patted my bottom and just pushed my face into her neck as she moved around the kitchen getting everything she needed for dinner. She eventually put me down on her couch and put a movie on, wrapping me in a fluffy blankie before she went back to finish making dinner.

"Here, little one, do you want to feed yourself," Vicki asked as she handed me my plate. I looked down and was impressed with what I saw.

"How did you know how to make something like this, Mommy?" I said, smelling the Asian dish she had made us.

"I told you I wasn't always a cop. I worked as a chef for a few years in Bali before I came back home and settled down here," Vicki said as I began to eat.

"This is delicious," I said. Vicki fed me the last few mouthfuls and patted my tummy.

"Full baby girl?" Vicki asked as I climbed into her arms and snuggled up on her with my blankie.

Chapter 7

The sun woke me before it did Vicki, and I looked down and touched the front of my diaper over the pink diaper cover Vicki had dressed me in. I was surprised I was so chill about playing along with this game she had going on. It felt nice to have someone care about me so much, to want to take away all the mean things that the world threw at me. I liked that I didn't have to do any of this grown-up stuff alone anymore. I thought back to yesterday, how she had been so patient and calm about me trying to push her away, instead of just bailing on me she had made me feel more loved than I had ever felt in my life.

I slowly got up and went out into the spacious living room and tried to turn the wall length TV on. Struggling to understand the table looking remote, I gave up and walked into the kitchen, where I saw a note saying that there were crackers and coloring ins on the table. I looked over and smiled, seeing the colors and books. Strolling over I sat down and flicked through the pages, seeing that they were empty. I liked that, I didn't want to share Mommy with anyone else, she was mine. I found a page I liked and began to color, humming to myself happily.

I was almost finished my page when I felt Vicki come up behind me and grab my waist in a hug.

"Good morning, baby girl," Vicki said, kissing my cheek and looking at my picture.

"Pretty little one, Mommy might have to rip it out and put in on the fridge," Vicki added, looking to see if I had eaten any of the crackers.

"Hi Mommy," I said, still focused on my drawing. I loved this, but it was Saturday, and I knew that Vicki was working tomorrow and didn't know when we would get my apartment cleaned.

"Mommy, maybe I should go and sort out my apartment?" I asked as she began to make breakfast. Vicki turned around and passed me a juice in my sippy cup.

"Baby, Mommy has already taken care of that. I have people there right now fixing it up," Vicki said, making me wonder when she had done all of that, and how she had done that. I looked at her, confused.

"So what, we just live happily ever after?" I said, unsure how to handle all this nice stuff that was happening. Vicki just laughed and nodded her head.

"That's kinda the idea, baby girl. Not everything has to be so hard," she said, cutting up my omelet and feeding me a mouthful. I ate silently, thinking about what happily ever after was meant to feel like. It was nice, but it was new, it was scary, and it was not something I knew how to live with. I so used to having to struggle, to hustle and be on constant guard that I couldn't understand how to drop that down and be at peace. I also didn't know how to tell Vicki any of this, so I just ate my breakfast and looked away from her.

"It's too good to be true Mommy, what gives?" I asked, feeling vulnerable for the first time. Vicki sat back and looked at me.

"You just got lucky baby girl, I didn't think that you'd hate this so much," Vicki said laughing and cleaning up our plates.

"I don't hate it; I don't know how to do this. Pretty suburban easy life with no drama, like what do you even do for fun?" I asked, shifting uncomfortably, wanting the diaper off.

"Come on, baby, let Mommy help you. Mommy's feisty little wild cat," Vicki said, winking at me, making me laugh.

"I heard them call you that once, and I thought how fitting it was for you," Vicki explained as she took off my diaper and passed me some big girl clothes.

"Can I still call you Mommy when I look like this?" I asked, feeling more comfortable and coming up to kiss Vicki full on her mouth.

"Yeah, baby girl, let's try for just nights in diapies, OK?" Vicki said, and I thought about it for a moment before nodding my head in agreement.

"I think I'd like that," I said, pulling on my tight pink tracksuit pants. I could tell Vicki liked how they looked, she wasn't even trying to hide her hardening dick and rubbed it opening in front of me.

"Mommy, do you like it?" I said, teasing her. I dropped to my knees and was surprised how excited I was to suck her. It was only the second time I'd had her in my mouth, but I swallowed her deeper than I had before.

"Oh Jesus baby girl, you're Mommy's little slut now aren't you," Vicki said, arching her back and shooting down my throat. She got up and ripped at my pants but stopped when I told her I was still too sensitive to have her there. She just smiled.

"We can work with that, let me play with you like this then," Vicki said as she rubbed her dick along my slit hitting my clit and teasing me.

Chapter 8

I stayed over at hers Saturday night, but come Sunday; I could tell she had work on her mind. She was less playful, and her energy was very controlling.

"What are you going to do today? I'll drop you home before work, Ava," Vicki said. I frowned when I had heard her say my name, and she noticed, coming over and grabbing hold of me.

"I have to be serious now baby, going out onto those streets is not a joke, I can't be feeling all lovely and Mommy right now. Do you understand?" Vicki explained, trying to sound like she had all weekend. I smiled and nodded, knowing that she was right; those streets were no joke.

We finished breakfast, and I packed my things away, explaining that I was going to look for a new apartment when I got home.

"Why don't you move in here?" Vicki said, taking me by surprise. She picked up my bag and walked to the door before I grabbed my wallet and keys and joined her.

"I don't know, do you think it's too soon?" I asked her nervously. She just shrugged.

"It's not like you won't be at mine every minute I'm not working anyway baby girl, Mommy owns you now, remember?"

Vicki said. I didn't like how controlling she was being. I had learned from a young age to take care of myself, and here she thought she was gods gift to the world.

"I still don't know," I said softly before suddenly feeling her hand on my thigh, prying my thighs apart and rubbing me roughly.

"It's not really up for discussion. You'll move in with me after my shift today, baby girl," Vicki said. I squirmed in my seat, which just made her laugh cruelly as she pulled my shorts to the side and forced a finger into my pussy.

"See how wet you are baby girl, don't try and tell Mommy you don't like this," Vicki said, pulling over to the side of the road and rubbing her dick wantonly. She pushed another finger into me and moved them inside of me. She reached into her pants and pulled her hard dick out, grabbing the back of my head and forcing herself into my mouth.

"Be Mommy's little fuck doll baby girl," Vicki moaned as she tilted her head back and closed her eyes as she used me. She worked her thumb over my clit and used her little finger to tease my ass, only stopping when I bit her. I couldn't think of anything else I could do to make her stop, and I was happy when it worked.

"Ouch you little bitch," Vicki said, pulling my head up and slapping me hard across my face. I looked at her, broken-hearted, and she changed back into my loving Mommy in an instant.

"I'm sorry, baby, I," was all I heard her say as I jumped out of her car, grabbed my backpack and ran down the street.

I knew she couldn't follow me as I jumped a fence down an alley and felt the familiar gravel tracks under my feet. I could feel the tears pouring down my face, but I didn't bother to stop them, I just kept running.

"Ava!" I heard her angrily yell, and I could tell she wasn't following me. I ran until I thought my lungs would give out and found myself in one of the old warehouses that I use to hide in when she would chase me for stealing something. I looked around the dirty place and was surprised I could have ever felt safe here. There were a couple of crack whores shooting up in the corner, and I decided that this wasn't going to be where I would stay. Leaving, I felt my legs take over, and I was running again, but this time, I knew where I was going home.

I hadn't seen my apartment since the night of the attack, and I was surprised just how well together it looked. After opening the door, I put my backpack down and looked around the space. Vicki hadn't lied when she said she'd take care of it. Looking down to see her ringing for the fifth time, I switched my phone off and went back to staring at my apartment. She had organized to have new furniture brought in, and it looked expensive and modern, like something from a luxury home magazine. She had artwork on the walls and had even put new appliances in the kitchen. There was a colorful rug in the living room, and she had even set up a new laptop and TV for me. She had bought me a new bed and had it dressed in pretty pink linen with two bunny's tucked into the middle of the bed. I went into the bathroom and was happy nothing had changed in there. She had bought me expensive shower gel and lotion, put sweet berry scented candles on the counter, and new hand towels. *Did she think I owed her? I never asked her for any of this,* I thought to myself, going back into the living room and sitting in front of my new laptop. It was the kind I could never afford, and I felt embarrassed and out of place in an apartment which I knew was mine, but that didn't feel like mine at all.

I got up and went to have a shower. After showering and enjoying the feel of the shower products on my skin, I looked in my cupboard to see that she had also bought me a selection of new clothes and shoes. Looking through the rack, I was happy she had left me with clothes I had bought but had to admit, she knew my style. I pulled on a pair of light denim, ripped jeans, and a light bubble gum pink t-shirt and went to make myself a cup of tea.

Turning my phone back on, I saw that she had called 12 times and sent three texts before I nervously read the messages. 'I am so sorry baby girl, please forgive me, it won't happen again, I don't know what came over me.' 'You are the most precious thing to me, please ring me back baby girl.' 'I hope you aren't scared of me now, Ava; I truly am so sorry, baby girl.' I was happy her messages weren't as angry as she was when I had left her. Deciding that I needed some time before I spoke to her again, I replied with, 'I am just going to need some time, I don't trust you anymore. Talk soon.' I didn't know how I was supposed to feel about this. I had been felt up heaps before, a couple of times it had even gone further than what she had done, but this was different. Maybe I was different. It hurt more, and I couldn't seem to brush it off. Maybe it was because I had let her in, and she had been the only person ever to make me feel safe, then for her to shatter that feeling of security was just too much. Or maybe it was because I had liked her and she wasn't just some punk with wandering hands. Deciding that it was all just too much, I lay down on my new couch, pulled my new blanket over me and fell asleep on my new cushions.

Chapter 9

I woke up to police sirens whirling down the street and blinked around my living room, wondering why it was so light. I didn't remember turning any lights on before I fell asleep, and I also didn't remember making any food, but the smell of Asian cooking made me instantly nervous. I quietly looked over the back of the couch to see Vicki standing in my kitchen, drinking a glass of red wine, and making dinner. She had on soft gray sweat shorts and a pink singlet, her hair down, and knee-high black socks.

"Vicki," I quietly said, making her turn around. I was scared of her, and she knew it. Her face going from happy to sad upon seeing the fear in my eyes.

"Baby girl, Mommy is so sorry," Vicki said, coming over and reaching of me. I flinched and pushed her hand away, pushing myself back to the edge of the couch. I was happy she looked hurt; she should be.

"How did you get in?" I asked sleepily. I could tell that I'd been asleep for hours by the hoarseness of my throat.

"I had a key cut when they fixed your apartment up," Vicki said, crossing her legs on the couch.

"I want you to leave," I said, looking down at my feet, they were cold. I stayed looking at them, I didn't want to look at her, she looked good, and I hated myself for finding her so wildly attractive when I was feeling so nervous about being around her. She took the blanket and put it over my toes and held them gently in her hands.

"Ava, I am sorry. You have to know that was an innocent mistake?" Vicki said lovingly. I looked at her as tears filled my eyes once more, and she moved closer to me, kicking my foot that I held up to try and stop her out of the way and pulled me into her arms.

"Just because you're stronger than me doesn't mean you can do that," I said, crying into her neck. I felt her arms tighten around me as she began to rock me.

"I trusted you," I added, looking up at her heartbroken. I was happy; she just nodded her head and didn't try to say anything. I could smell the dinner slightly burning, and I wriggled out of her embrace, happy she let me and went to the kitchen. I turned the wok off and stayed there looking at it as I felt her move behind me and drape her arms over my shoulders.

"I know you did, you still can. I didn't think your no was a no, and I'm sorry," Vicki said. For the first time, I saw how vulnerable she really was, and I liked that I felt like I was talking to the real her.

"I still want you to go, I need some time Vicki," I said. I could see she was hurt by me calling her by her name, but I was glad she just nodded her head and started to collect her things.

"Just add the noodles if you want, everything is ready," Vicki said as she put her shoes on, left her key by the door, and walked out.

I hadn't heard from her for a week before I felt like I could breathe easy again. I had stopped feeling like she was watching me, and I even started going for jogs again around the park. I had worked the usual 9-5 at the furniture store and had got myself into a routine of cooking every night instead of just ordering out. Things were going well. I missed her, though, but I knew that that would pass soon enough as well. I had even set up a couple of dates with some girls online to try and shake her out of my system. One of those dates was tonight.

I had tried the usual dating sites, mostly because I'm lazy and didn't want to get off my couch and also because it's just hard to find girls in the hood who don't have kids, a convict record or some kind of addiction. But I had narrowed my search down to this one girl who seemed really nice. Her name was Melanie, and she lived in the same area as me. She had shoulder-length blonde hair and a sweet smile, so when she asked me out for dinner at a local restaurant I figured it would be a nice time. I got dressed in a short red dress and pulled on cream heels, touching up my makeup before I left my building.

Walking down the block, I saw the usual working girls, a few pimps looking out the window of the diners that were scattered up the street and our local homeless man who always told me how pretty I was. I liked him and would buy him cream buns or coffee most afternoons after work, and he had chased away more than one guy who had mistaken me for one of the streetwalkers. I couldn't blame them. These guys weren't from around here, and every girl in a dress looked the same to them. But to us, we were worlds apart. For one, I looked fed, I didn't have that hungry, will fuck for food or pills kind of vibe, and I looked like I had somewhere to be. As I passed one clearly new girl, she bumped shoulders with me accidentally.

"Oh, I'm so sorry, are you OK?" She asked. She had dropped her wallet, and I reached down to pick it up for her. She had sad runaway eyes and a painted smile, and I wondered what they'd get her addicted to so they could keep her. She looked like a runner.

"Yeah, I'm fine, stay safe," I said as I handed her wallet back just as her pimp came out of a diner. I could tell she was hers by the way she quickly walked to us.

"I'm going, I just bumped her making her drop her stuff," I said, putting my hands up in defense. I had learned not to mess with these guys.

"Yo, Ava, we're all good," she said. Growing up here, you ended up knowing everyone.

"Still fucking that cop?" She added. I didn't know who she

was, but she certainly knew me. Playing it cool, I spat on the ground.

"Fuck the police," I said, making her laugh, and we pounded fists as I walked off, happy to be out of there. *You did fuck the police;* I thought to myself in amusement as I entered the restaurant I was meeting Melanie at. I looked around and saw her sitting at the bar waiting for me. *Cute,* I thought, seeing her black dress and pink heels. I made my way over to her and sat down next to her.

"Hi," she said, looking over to me.

"Hi, wow, your photos don't really do you justice," I said to her, making her laugh. We paid for our drinks and made our way to the table by the window. I was aware that there were a number of cops walking the street tonight. They were in plain clothes, but growing up here, we learned to see a cop before we learned how to count to ten.

"I'm really glad you took me up on this date Ava, not many people I've spoken to have been as interesting as you," Melanie said. I laughed, she was trying so hard, and I liked having someone practically beg for me.

"I wouldn't be here if you hadn't told me about how you captured those aerial shots over the river. They were so beautiful, you're right, drones are the future of photography," I said. The waiter came over, and we ordered our dinner as we continued to talk. She told me about the other photo series she had taken and how she sold them online. I told her about how I had to start again after my gear got stolen, and she offered to lend me her equipment over the weekend. I had just finished my dinner when an angry police officer walked in and stood by our table. At first, I didn't pay any attention to her. I had assumed that she was looking at someone else, not us.

"Ma'am, I'm going to need you to step outside with me," she said, stopping our conversation. We both looked at each other before Melanie quickly jumped up and sprinted past the cop who reached for her taser but stopped when I got up, grabbing me firmly and pulling me to her before turning me around and walking me out the door.

"What the fuck, let me go, you fat fuck," I said, struggling against her grip. I could tell she was going to leave bruises on my arms.

"Had to wait until I wasn't running to get me, huh," I said. The cop was obviously not in the mood for my sass as she flung me against her car, winding me, making me cough and moan in pain.

"Well, well haven't you grown up little Ava Meadows," the cop said, reaching around and patting me down over my tits. I hated that she knew me. I hated that she had the 'right' to touch me. I also hated that I knew even if I stopped resisting her, she would still be as rough and grabby as she was now. I had tried that, just doing what they wanted without a fight, but the result was always the same around here. They'd cop a feel and force it on you regardless of how well mannered you were, so you might as well try to get them off if you could.

Chapter 10

"Get off of me," I yelled, struggling against the cops weight. She pulled me back just to push me against the car again and kicked my feet out, making me spread my legs. Pinning me down, I could feel my lungs being crushed, and I gasped for air. I could feel her hands on me, reaching around and patting me down just as my eyes closed and my head went dizzy. Just before I passed out, I felt her reaching up my thighs before being pulled away, and the sudden fullness of my lungs made my legs buckle. Strong hands held me up, and I knew whose touch was on me now instantly.

"Vicki," I said softly, feeling my head spin, and her hands take over the search. She was gentle; there wasn't the hate in her touch like there was in the first cops, and I moved my body to her instructions.

"Turn around for me," Vicki said affectionately. I slowly brought my feet together before I turned very slowly to face her. It was the first time I had seen her in a month, and she frowned as she saw the gash across my cheek.

"Be more careful next time," Vicki aggressively said to her partner, who just huffed and kicked the dirt. Vicki placed her hand under my chin and moved my neck as she ran her fingers through my hair. She placed both her hands on my stomach as she felt down my front and whispered that it was OK when she felt me whimper as she ran her hands down my thighs. I could feel the blood from my cheek run down my face, and Vicki took out a tissue and offered it to me kindly. I gladly accepted and pressed against my face, grimacing with the pain.

"We are still going to need you to come down to the station Ava; we need to ask you a few questions," Vicki said. I could see in her eyes she wasn't in cop mode, and I liked how she was talking to me. It was soft and kind and didn't make me feel worried.

"Hands behind your back," the other cop said, grabbing my upper arm and spinning me around and pressing me hard against the car again. Vicki grabbed her shoulder and pulled her back, spinning me around and half holding me to her side.

"She doesn't need them," she said, glaring down the other cop and subtly patted me on the back. It took all my strength not to snuggle into her. I could feel her hot breath on me and her protective stance, and it made me realize how much I had missed her. I liked that I could tell she had missed me too and I smiled at her weakly as she opened the car door for me.

At the station, it looked as though nothing had changed in years. The rooms were just as cold, and the cops were just as noisy. Vicki walked me to a room at the end of a corridor and got me a cup of coffee while I waited. I looked around the room; it felt funny being back in here. At least this time I knew I wasn't in any actual trouble. The cop who had interrupted my date came in first and slammed some folders down on the table. *Why did they always do that?* I thought to myself, watching her try and be assertive. *I shall name you, Constable fuckface,* I thought adamantly, smirking to myself.

"So you know Ms. Hunter?" She said. I looked at her and wondered if she was this angry because she never got laid.

"Not really, I met her online, and we went out for dinner tonight before you guys jumped us," I replied. I didn't mind being honest with her, I was definitely not about to see Melanie again, and I didn't owe her anything.

"Where did you meet?" Constable fuckface asked. Flicking through the files, she placed multiple pictures of dead girls in front of me.

"Online," I replied, looking down at the photos she was showing me.

"This is who you really met. A drug mule who is known for recruiting over dating apps. Do you do drugs, Ms. Meadows?" She asked as Vicki walked into the room. I could tell she had heard what I had said about meeting Melanie online by her sad expression.

"No, I don't do drugs," I said, looking at Vicki.

"Try to focus on Ms. Meadows. She can't help you now, you've made a right mess for yourself," the cop said, sounding impressed with herself. Vicki sat down and leaned back in the chair, crossing her arms over her chest.

"How long where you talking with her?" Vicki asked. I could tell she was not asking for any reason connected to this case.

"Only two weeks," I replied, enjoying ignoring the other cop who was obviously mad that Vicki had taken over.

"Did she ever say anything about her work?" The other cop said, trying to gain control again. I death stared her before reaching into my clutch and pulling out my phone. I slid it across the table towards Vicki, who grabbed it without looking away from me.

"You can read the messages; I was hardly in love with the girl. We talked about photography and growing up around here. She invited me to dinner, it's not like I was doing anything anyway," I said as Vicki held the phone. Silence fell between the three of us before the other cop broke it.

"That'll be all for tonight, Ms. Meadows. Lovely to see you again, I'll let Constable Smith show you out, although I'm sure you remember the way," the cop said, leaving the room. Vicki and I just stayed sitting there. She spun my phone on the cold metal table, and I watched as the clock ticked by.

"I'm not mad," Vicki finally spoke.

"Not here," I said, standing up, wanting to leave. Vicki nodded and got up, handing me my phone back. We walked in silence out of the station, constable fuckface was right, I did remember my way out. It was near midnight, and the air was cold as I kicked my foot along the sidewalk, I was hoping Vicki would be finished her shift soon.

"You'll need this," I said, turning to her and placing her spare key in her hand. Vicki looked down, and I could see her heart almost jump out of her chest, and she inhaled deeply. She looked at me with a surprised look, and I smiled.

"Don't make a fool out of me. I can forgive once, but never twice, Vicki," I said, feeling in control of my life for the first time. Vicki went to hug me but stopped herself, looking around to see if there was someone else out here with us. Nodding her head at another cop who walked past she gave me a sideward smile before speaking.

"I'll never hurt you again, Ava," Vicki quietly whispered. I could tell she meant it, too, which made me happy.

"Come home to me tonight? I've missed you," I asked Vicki, who nodded her head.

"Let me drive you home, or call you a cab, whatever you want," Vicki said. She was right, it was probably too late to be walking the streets, and it was far too cold. I hadn't brought a jacket, and my arms were stone cold.

I waited inside to wait for the cab Vicki had called me, and she walked me down to tell the driver where to take me.

"Make sure she gets home safely," she said in her angry

cop voice before placing her hand gently on my cheek and stroking me with her thumb.

"See you soon," Vicki said affectionately before paying the driver and closing the door. The cab driver looked at me in the backseat, but I was happy he didn't say a word the whole drive home. I also knew he'd done jail time by his crude tattoos and wondered how he felt about taking the girl of a cop home. People knew not to mess with Vicki, and it felt good knowing I had her reputation to protect me again. When we got to my building, the driver got out of the car and walked me to the building door.

"You'll be alright, miss?" He asked, accepting my tip.

"Yeah, thanks," I said, going inside. The truth was, I was a little scared, but I really didn't want him knowing where I lived. I'd had enough dramas in this apartment for a while.

It was early morning when I heard Vicki unlock the door and creep into the house. She dropped her gear, and I could tell she had showered at work. Her hair was a little bit damp but smelt like sweet strawberry hair products as she climbed into bed with me. I could tell she wasn't sure how close she was allowed next to me, so I rolled over and put her mind at ease. I climbed on top of her and rested my head on her chest, happy when she wrapped her arms around me and relaxed.

"I've missed you, baby girl," Vicki whispered in my ear as she stroked my hair and patted my ass. I loved feeling her again and snuggled into her body, falling back asleep safe again in her arms.

Chapter 11

"This is weird. Does it feel weird to you?" I asked Vicki the minute her eyes opened the next morning. I had been watching her sleep and playing with her hair, and she smiled, kissing me before she opened her eyes.

"Why does it feel weird?" Vicki said, sitting up and stretching as she yawned. I curled up into her and waited for her arm to find its way back around me before I spoke.

"Because, like, last night and the last months, and now you're laying in my bed, and I feel so happy I could just punch you," I replied.

"You could punch me?" Vicki questioned.

"Yeah, you're the only woman I've ever wanted, and I hated you so much for making me so sad, and now I feel like I was in hell before right now," I explained. Vicki jumped up and kneeled on the bed, spreading her arms out wide.

"Then punch me," she said. I looked at her questioningly.

"If that's what it will take for you to be happy with me again, punch me," Vicki said, smirking.

"Don't laugh just because you know my punch won't hurt you," I said, looking down at her dick.

"No, this doesn't turn me on, it's just what happens in the

morning," Vicki said as if reading my mind.

"Punching you won't hurt you, but this will," I said as I kneed her dick. Grabbing herself and looking like she was about to vomit, Vicki fell down on the bed and breathed in labored breaths.

"Even?" Vicki asked, tears rolled down her face. I felt bad for about half a second.

"Even," I said, kissing her cheek and holding her until she could move again.

"So, how are we going to do this?" Vicki asked over breakfast. She had made buttermilk pancakes, and I had eaten more than my stomach could hold and lay in a food coma on the couch.

"I think we just lay here until breathing doesn't hurt anymore," I replied, closing my eyes. Vicki laughed as she came over with a cup of coffee and sat by my side.

"I meant us little one," Vicki said, bending down to kiss my tummy. I opened my eyes and reached up to cuddle her, getting tickled by her hair.

"I don't know. I don't want to move in together straight away, though," I replied. Vicki smiled and began stroking my hair, and I could feel the little space beginning to take hold. Vicki must have noticed too because she lay down next to me and began cuddling my body.

"I figured that much baby girl," she said, wrapping her arm around my head as she pushed her tits into my face. I loved the feel of them, the heaviness, and her thick nipples. I could tell she was fighting herself; I could tell what she wanted by the look in her eyes and smirking back at her cheekily, I pulled on her nipple through her shirt.

"Want to play little one?" Vicki said as I nodded my head. She pulled out her full breast, and I sucked her nipple immediately, enjoyed the throaty moan that involuntarily escaped Vicki as she pushed her nipple into my mouth.

"Mommy has missed this little mouth, baby girl," Vicki said, making me smile around her nipple.

"I think we should sit down and come up with some rules and lay a foundation for what our limits are baby girl, what do you think?" Vicki asked, taking her nipple from my reach. I knew that we should do this, but I didn't want to do it now, I wanted to have her now. I reluctantly watched as she put her breast back into her shirt before I went to get a notepad and pen.

"Ok, so, ground rules, give the baby everything she wants, all the time," I said cheekily as Vicki came to sit at the kitchen table with me. She rolled her eyes and took the pen and pad away from me.

"I don't think so," she said, crossing out my first rule.

"Let's start with the important one, safe words," Vicki said, eyeing me. I nodded and thought before I spoke.

"Let's just do traffic lights, green for go, yellow for slow down and red for stop; they are easy to remember," I said as Vicki wrote it down agreeing.

"I only want to tell you an instruction once," Vicki said, writing that down too.

"I don't want to be used as a fuck doll," I said, looking Vicki dead in the eye.

"You have to ask permission before you fuck me, I'm yours, but I'm not just open for business," I added. I like that Vicki agreed to that one, I had been worried she wouldn't. We kept going, creating rules and frameworks, punishments, and expectations well into the afternoon.

"Come on, baby girl, let's go outside before the whole day is over," Vicki said, picking me up and carrying me into the bedroom. She placed me down on the bed before she grabbed my jeans and a diaper. We had agreed she could diaper me if I was wearing jeans and I smiled at how she let me decide which one I wanted.

"I haven't worn these since last time, Mommy," I said, referring to the last time she had diapered me. Vicki smiled happily.

"Good," she said, pulling my jeans up over my diaper. She passed me a pink bra and almost see-through pink blouse, and Vicki took my hands away to do up the buttons herself.

"Let Mommy baby girl," she said, groping my tits when

she was finished.

"You are so beautiful, baby," Vicki whispered in my ear, and I knew she wanted to fuck me. I liked that she actually always wanted to fuck me, and I kissed her deeply while she rubbed my diaper and jeans covered ass. It felt so good that I moved on top of her thigh and straddled it, rocking back and forth on her as she let me dry hump her leg.

"Baby girl, Mommy needs to get ready," Vicki said playfully, throwing me down on the bed and grabbing my tits one last time before she went to freshen up. I lay on the bed and watched her as she brushed her teeth and ran her fingers through her hair. I liked that she had taken her top off and walked around the room with just her pants on. She saw me staring at her, and she winked at me before finding the shirt she wanted and putting it on.

"Ready?" Vicki said, taking my hand and pulling me to her. She kissed down my neck and picked me up, turning me around and pinning me against a wall. I kissed her, feeling her hands on my sides and making me hold my breath as she enveloped me.

"Ready," I breathlessly said, slightly annoyed when she put me back down again.

We walked out of my building and to her car.

"Get in," she said, making me wonder where we were going. I opened the door and waited for her to buckle me in like we had discussed, kissing her on the mouth when she did so.

"Where are we going Mommy," I said feeling Vicki move her hand to cup the front of my pussy. I wriggled and pushed it out, making her smile as she patted me like her pet.

"To a place, I think you'll like baby girl," Vicki replied, turning into my favorite fast food restaurant and buying me a shake and small fries. Vicki ordered three hamburgers, and I laughed at how much she could eat. I liked that she took her time eating them. I was worried she'd get a tummy ache.

"I'm starving, I only had six pancakes for breakfast," Vicki said, catching me looking at her.

"I only had 2!" I giggled. Vicki played with my hair as she turned the corner, her forearm flexing.

"These muscles don't grow by themselves, baby girl," Vicki added, making me curious.

"Don't you just go to the gym and bam, muscles?" I asked. Vicki looked at me like she couldn't figure out if I was serious or not.

"No...we can get into my gym schedule later. We are here," Vicki said, parking the car. I looked around, she had taken us to a spot out of town, and I smiled, noticing that there were no other cars in the parking lot.

"Out you come," Vicki said, unbuckling me and lifting me out of her SUV. I went to grab my backpack, but she slung it over her shoulder and held my hand as we began walking along a hiking path.

"It's so lovely, Mommy," I said, enjoying being outside and alone with Vicki. She smiled and looked down at me.

"I use to come here for runs when I didn't want anyone around. Look," she said, pointing to a bird's nest with a mama bird feeding her baby birds.

"Pretty Mommy," I said, standing on my tippy toes to get a closer look. Vicki smiled and walked ahead of me, turning around when I didn't follow her and held out her hand to me.

"Come on, sweetie," she said, smiling as I ran to catch up to her. We continued walking for an hour until we reached the edge of a cliff and the view took my breath away. Looking out over a cliff, there was a waterfall to the right of us, and in front of us, there was nothing but the silhouette of the city we had left behind. The sun was about an hour from setting, and Vicki laid out a blanket and began unpacking the picnic she had made.

"You know, I could get used to this," I said, laying down and resting my head on her thigh. Vicki took my hands in hers as she poured anti-bacteria gel over them and washed them clean before passing me a sandwich.

"Good baby girl, this is the life Mommy wants to have with you," Vicki replied, putting me in my little space. Her hair was being swept up gently by the breeze and every now, and then the water from the waterfall would sprinkle on us, making me giggle. Vicki kept me laying down and put a paci in my mouth after we had finished our picnic, laughing when I looked at her with wide eyes.

"Don't worry about girl, I'll hear if someone is coming and you can give it back to Mommy, but right now, it's either your paci or Mommy, which one?" Vicki said, raising an eyebrow at me. I touched my paci, and Vicki brought me into her lap and wrapped her arms around me as I enjoyed the warm sun on my face, watching rainbows form in the waterfall.

Chapter 12

Vicki and I had picnics at our special spot for the next three weeks. We had spent most of the time at my apartment, but I had slept over at hers for a few nights at a time before I wanted to go back home. I was happy that she had been true to her word and not broken our contract, and I had totally forgotten that anything wrong could ever happen in the world. That was until I got a phone call from an old friend.

"Hey, where you at?" Came a familiar voice down the phone.

"Rory?" I asked, surprised she would have my number.

"Yeah, who else. Look I'm out, can I meet you somewhere?" She said. I had met Rory when we had been kids. She lived on the same block as me and had taken the wrap for me the first time I got caught by Vicki. She was a quiet kid, the kind who came up with ideas but had lost almost every fight she had ever been in. I had heard she had been away, got caught stealing a car from a wealthy lawyer the day after she turned 18 and had been tried as an adult. She'd gotten 10years, but I guess she was out early for good behavior or something.

"Yo, you there?" Rory said, breaking my train of thought.

"Yeah, sorry. Where are you?" I replied. She gave me the

address, and I knew that I could probably get there and back before Vicki got home. She was coming to mine tonight to stay over, but I still had a few hours before she'd be here, so I told Rory to meet me at a diner around the corner from mine and said I'd meet her there.

I had only been waiting for five minutes before I saw her come in, but without the scar on her face, I wouldn't have even recognized her. She was bigger, and her head was shaved. She walked with a limp and had really aggressive energy. *I guess she did just get out of prison,* I thought to myself, watching her walk over to me. People were looking at her fearfully, and she just looked back them, not seeming to mind.

"Hey there, wild cat," Rory said, looking me up and down. I got up to hug her, but she just sat down. I guess those sorts of things were lost on her now.

"You some sort of office broad now?" She said, accepting the free coffee from the waitress.

"You hungry?" I said, ignoring her tease, she just shrugged her shoulders, and I ordered two big all-day breakfasts before the waitress left.

"So?" Rory said, looking around. I looked around to thinking that something was going on. However, there was nothing out of the ordinary.

"So," I repeated, sipping my coffee.

"You got a man?" Rory said. I could see she was trying to

make conversation, but it didn't feel like the old times. She had tattoos down the side of her face and on her knuckles. I don't think anyone would even enter into a fight with her these days.

"I'm gay," I said, shaking my head, making Rory instantly excited.

"Alright, I always knew there was a reason I liked ya. Not many of us around here back then. What's it like now, get a bitch easy hey," Rory said as the waitress placed our meals in front of us. I wasn't really sure how I could reply to her without getting a punch in my face. I wasn't about to say I was in love with a cop.

"Yeah, look last time I went on a date with a girl she turned out to be a drug mule, so," I chose instead, making Rory laugh.

"You still rolling with Hope and them?" Rory said, hunching over her food and making me wonder how many times she had her food taken away in there. She was almost annalistic.

"No, actually. I stepped away from all of that. Got myself a steady job and all of it," I decide to say, not wanting her to think I was about that kind of living anymore.

"Good girl," Rory said, making me surprised my body reacted the way it did. Instantly I got a usual throbbing between my thighs, and I looked at her in shock. She was a far cry from anything I found attractive, and yet my cunt was immediately on fire. Swallowing hard, I pushed my plate away, knowing that I wouldn't be able to stomach anymore.

"You done?" Rory said, pointing to my plate. I nodded, and she switched plates and began finishing off my half-finished food. Looking at my watch, I knew that Vicki would be home in an hour.

"Where are you staying?" I asked Rory hoping that she wouldn't try and bunk down with me. I had long stopped taking in strays.

"Here and there. I'm good though, I don't need your help, I just wanted to see ya, pretty little thing," Rory said making me bite my lip which just made her laugh.

"You got me through, you know," Rory said, sitting back in the booth and signaling to the waitress she wanted more coffee. I knew what she meant, but I really wished I didn't, so playing dumb, I gave her an opportunity to change her story.

"What do you mean?" I said, shaking my head at the waitress who offered me coffee.

"Yeah, she will actually," Rory said, calling her back and ordering for me.

"But I don't want it," I said to Rory, annoyed that I could feel my little voice coming out, which just seemed to excite her.

"I know you don't, but you'll take it and give it to me instead, see," Rory said, drinking from my cup. I watched her drink, her eyes never breaking from mine.

"I have to go," I said, standing up, but being blocked by her. She stood in my way and grabbed my hips.

"Always such a pretty girl, I meant it what I said, you got me through. Thinking about you, the way you laughed as you ran, your tanned legs dodging the cops. You should be with me since you ain't got no one. You're too little to protect yourself, always have been. It was always me who looked after you," Rory said. I hated how she was making me feel. Her eyes had become soft, but I wondered how mean she would turn when I turned her down.

"Rory," I said, taking her hands away, happy when she let me. I looked at her and tried to stay calm, but my heart was pounding, and I had to fight myself not to run away from her.

"I'm glad you're out, but I really do need to go," I repeated. She smiled and nodded to the floor, letting me pass.

"I'll be seeing ya," Rory said as I left the diner, making me turn my head and look plainly at her. *Am I just some fucking slut that'll let any Mommy fuck her?* I thought to myself as I quickly made my way back to my apartment.

"Baby girl?" Vicki said as I entered the apartment. I dropped my bag and jumped into her arms; happy, her reflexes were so acute. She held me as I wrapped my arms around her neck, pushing myself into her and kissing her deeply. She moaned in my mouth as she grabbed the top of my jeans and broke the kiss looking for my consent.

"Yeah, fuck me, Mommy," I said, nodding and kissing her neck and along her shoulder. Vicki didn't need to be told twice, walking to the couch and throwing me down, dropping to her knees as I bounced on the couch. She grabbed my shirt and pulled it off, moaning when she saw I wasn't wearing a bra and kissing my tits and down my tummy making me wriggle under her. She unbuttoned the multiple buttons of my jeans in one go and ripped them off, smiling in primal satisfaction when she saw my diaper.

"Oh good girl, baby," she moaned, seeing that I kept her rules even when she wasn't there to enforce them. She reached under my arms and picked me up and took me to the bedroom, carrying me with one arm while her other one pulled her belt off her trousers. She placed me gently down on the bed and turned me over, before placing one hand on the middle of my back and belting my ass with her belt. She knew that I needed my diaper on when I was belted, she was just too strong, and it just hurt way too much. I liked that I could trust her again. She belted my ass until I was just about to call it off before ripping off my diaper and undoing her trousers. Her dick was hard, and when she ran it between my ass cheeks, I enjoyed her moaning as she came instantly, slipping the tip of her dick into my ass, squirting down inside of me.

"Holy shit, baby girl, you get Mommy excited," Vicki said, drying her dick off with her trousers before spitting on her hand and rubbing it over my aching cunt. I knew I was wet; I'd been wet since I was with Rory. I pushed the image of Rory out of my mind as I felt Vicki spread my pussy wide and enter me forcefully. I loved that she never fucked around when it came to fucking. She grabbed my hips and buried her dick inside of me, holding it in me as she squirted into me before she began thrusting against my red ass.

"Tell Mommy you need it, baby girl," Vicki said as she pounded me from behind. She reached around and rubbed my clit as she sat back and bounced me on her lap, making me take her dick hard.

"Mommy, I need you, please fuck me, Mommy," I said, closing my eyes and opening them suddenly as the image of Rory standing in front me playing with herself entered my mind as Vicki fucked me until she was coming for the third time.

"I'm not done with you yet," Vicki said in a tone I had heard multiple times. She pulled out of me and slapped my face with her dick before going to my cupboard and taking out a bondage rope and nipple clamps. I looked at her warningly making her laugh.

"I know the rules baby girl, Mommy isn't going to hurt you, you're going to love this," Vicki said as she grabbed my wrists and tied them to my ankles. I was happy she did, in fact, know the rules and left my throat untied. She rolled me over and flicked my nipples until they were hard and clamped them before going back into the cupboard and taking out my black bunny butt plug.

"Mommy, no," I said, smiling. Vicki raised an eyebrow seeing that I wasn't really asking her to stop and stuck the plug into my pussy, making it wet before pushing it into my resisting ass.

"You've always got to fight Mommy on something, don't you baby girl?" Vicki teased as she guided herself back into me, making me scream in pleasure.

"I told you you'd like it. Mommy's pretty little slut," Vicki said as she held my shoulders and rammed into me until my eyes rolled back and I shut my eyes.

"Tell Mommy where I can finish baby girl," Vicki moaned, edging herself. My pussy juices were squirting out onto her pelvis, and Vicki pulled out of me, jerking herself, waiting for my answer.

"You can put it in my mouth, Mommy," I said as Vicki quickly filled my mouth. I hadn't had her down my throat at this angle before, and she slid down deeper than I had ever taken her. She moaned as she came in my mouth, rubbing my throat and smiling as she felt her dick deep inside of it.

"Baby girl," she said, cupping my chin and gently pulling out of me. I swallowed one more time, and Vicki reached over, passing me a water bottle, laughing when she realized I was tied.

"Let me, sweetie," she said, bringing the bottle to my lips and letting me drink. She untied me, and I lay spent on the bedsheets that were now covered in cum and sweat.

"That was the best sex we've ever had," Vicki said, picking me up and taking me into the bathroom. I just nodded and relaxed in her arms as she bathed me.

"I love you, Vicki," I said sleepily. I closed my eyes and heard her smile as she replied.

"I love you too, Ava; you're my whole world."

Chapter 13

"I didn't think it could be true when I heard, but I guess you are a sell-out after all," I heard Rory say, as I walked up the street. I knew this wasn't going to end well, and I slowly turned around to see her angry face. I had been right; it was terrifying.

"Fucking a cop, low bitch, real low," Rory said. I looked around, hoping that she didn't have anyone with her.

"I can't help who I fall in love with Rory," I said softly. Clearly pissed off, Rory started shaking her head and looking around, moving from one foot to another.

"Na see, I don't believe that. You had a choice; you chose them over us. I had even defended you bitch, told them they were talking wack, but I seen you too, holding hands, kissing," Rory said as if she was talking about the most disgusting thing on the planet. I stood there, looking at her weighing up my options. I could run, but I had a sneaky feeling she could catch me despite her size. I knew I couldn't fight her, and I knew that no one was going to help me if she threw a punch.

"Rory, I'm sorry it's upset you, but," I started to say, getting cut off by her shaking her hand in my face.

"She's got a cock, you know, didn't know you was into that, fucking a freak she's not even a real woman," Rory said, making the biggest mistake she could have. I burned with rage and swung at her, surprising her and myself as I slammed into her face making her stumble. She looked at me before spitting a mouthful of blood out onto the sidewalk.

"Oh, you asked for this bitch," she said, swinging back and slugging me in the guts. I doubled over, stepping back, trying to escape her.

"Learnt a couple of things while I was away," Rory said, punching me again, this time coming down on my back.

"First thing is you either ride or die and guess what baby girl, you just tapped out," Rory said, pulling my hair back and punching me in my eye socket. I fell to the ground just as she stamped on my leg and getting up; I tried to run from her. I got about ten paces until she had me with my arm locked behind my back and pushing me into an alley. I knew what was going to come next and thought of Vicki, trying to get wet to make it hurt less.

"I'm going to enjoy this," Rory said, reaching up my skirt and pulling my panties down. I screamed before she had done anything, only resulting in getting turned around and punched in my stomach, but it was too late.

"You're fucked bitch, you couldn't have me then, you couldn't even have me now," I said as I spat a mouthful of blood at her hearing Vicki's unmistakable footsteps racing down the alley.

"Oi, come here," Vicki yelled in her angry cop voice as she chased Rory and slammed her to the ground, pinning her head down as she cuffed her wrists behind her.

"Ava, can you hear me," Constable fuckface gently said, shining a torch in my face.

"Yeah," I replied softly.

"I'll put her in the back, you stay with Ava," I heard Vicki say as I passed out in Constable fuckface's arms.

When I woke up again, I was in the hospital. I knew it was hospital by that distinctive hospital smell. A nurse was looking at something on the monitor when I made a soft sound that I was happy she heard.

"Welcome back," she said before leaving the room again.

"Baby girl," Vicki said, rushing in obviously the nurse had told her I was awake. Vicki stroked my hair and kissed my forehead, making me smile and cough.

"Shh, it's OK, sweetie, you don't have to talk. Mommy's here," Vicki said. I tried to touch my eye, but there was something covering it.

"You'll have to have that on for a little while baby girl, you're eye socket is a little broken. The woman who did this to you, you knew her?" Vicki said. I nodded and heard a person clear their throat behind Vicki.

"You know I have to ask the questions Victoria,"

Constable fuckface said, making Vicki roll her eyes.

"But I hate you," I said softly, making Vicki laugh.

"Yes, well, I'd hate me too if I was you wild cat," she said, making me laugh.

"Tell me what happened. Why are you always getting into trouble?" She added as I got up, helped by Vicki.

"I knew her from way back. She got done for stealing a car and got out recently. I went to see her," I said, looking at Vicki.

"I'm sorry I didn't tell you, I just kinda didn't want to bring you into that world, it's shit," I said apologetically. Vicki just laughed.

"Baby, I'm in this world every day," she said, frowning when I shook my head.

"Na is different when you come from it, Victoria," I said, enjoying calling her by her real name. She raised an eyebrow at me, making it very clear that would the only tease I would be getting away with.

"And then what happened, you met up with her and then what?" The other cop pressed.

"She was keen on me, said it was me who got her through her time, but I said I wasn't in that world anymore. I saw her again today, she started talking shit and then," I said, stopping to look at Vicki. I was pretty sure people would know at her work, but I still wasn't sure, and I didn't want to out her if no one knew.

"She started saying some shit about you, and that's when

I punched her," I said.

"What did she say?" The other cop said, making me look nervously at Vicki, who just smiled lovingly.

"It's OK, baby girl," she said, bending down and kissing me.

"She said you were a freak and not a real woman, so I slugged her," I said, my little voice coming out and resulting in Vicki bending down cuddle me.

"You're a cute little girl for defending Mommy baby girl," Vicki whispered in my ear, making me feel proud.

"You sure took a beating for that baby," she said louder, standing back up and going over to Constable fuckface who was busy jotting down my story.

"Charge her for attempted rape, Jane," Vicki said.

"Jane?" I said questioningly. Jane nodded her head before she bopped me on the nose with her notepad.

"But what's it to you?" She said, making me laugh.

"I may call you constable, only constable," I replied, repeating what she had made me say countless times before. Vicki smiled, almost enjoying watching me be controlled by someone else and sat on the bed when Jane had gone.

"Really to go home, little baby?" She asked. I nodded my head and let her help me up.

"Cops are such control freaks," I said, making Vicki laugh.

"Um, yeah, that's kinda the point," she added, wrapping

an arm around me and helping me walk out of the hospital.

"Mommy!" I said four months later as Vicki placed the big painting I had just finished on the wall. I had moved into her house a couple of months ago and had happily gotten used to my new suburb in the nice part of town. It hadn't been as hard as I had thought it would be hanging out in Vicki's world, and I had enjoyed starting to meet her friends, and she had even started to meet mine from the furniture store. I had been given the promotion I put in for which meant I could move to a store closer to our home and had bought a drone to take photos over the waterfall Vicki and I seemed to spend most of our spare time at.

"Looks good doesn't it baby girl," Vicki said. I sat in front of it and was happy with how I had designed it. The pinks and gold leaf had been constructed to represent a heart that had been broken and put back together; the broken pieces merging to create an even bigger heart than the original was.

"Snackies, baby girl?" Vicki said, picking me up and covering me in kisses as she bought me into the kitchen and took out the pizza we had made together. She had two, I finally understood her food and gym schedule, and she had let me use cookie cutters to cut mine into different shapes.

"This is nice, Mommy," I said, using the tongs to put my dino pizzas on one side of my plate and the teddy pizzas on the other side. I held my plate in two hands and beamed up at her deeply impressed with myself.

"I love you, baby girl," Vicki said, beaming back down at me.

Who is Tina Moore?

Tina Moore has enjoyed the lifestyle of a Mommy Domme for several years. She began exploring kink and BDSM in her youth and found her love of being a strict Mommy Domme in early 2000. Tina Moore is now an author of many MDLG and ABDL themed novels.

Having enjoyed many years in the kink community, Tina Moore combines these experiences with the sweet and naughty things her baby girl does to bring you tantalizing and salacious stories.

Follow her on:

Author Page on Amazon

Instagram @tinamoore.kdp